To Yunhee

Henry in Love. Copyright © 2010 by Peter McCarty. Manufactured in China.

Library of Congress Cataloging-in-Publication Data is available.
ISBN 978-0-06-114288-8 (trade bdg.) — ISBN 978-0-06-114289-5 (lib. bdg.)

The art for this book was done on Fabriano 140 lb. hot press watercolor paper
with Sennelier shellac-based colored inks and Winsor and Newton watercolors.

Typography by Martha Rago
10 11 12 13 14 LEO 10 9 8 7 6 5 4 3 2 1 ❖ First Edition

HENRY IN LOVE

Peter McCarty

Balzer + Bray
An Imprint of HarperCollins*Publishers*

Henry awoke to the smell of blueberry muffins.

He got ready for the day

and headed downstairs to the kitchen.

For breakfast Henry and his brother, Tim,

had cereal, toast, a banana, and a glass of juice.

"The blueberry muffins are for school,"
said their mother.

"Can I have one too, Mrs. Calico?"
asked Henry's friend Sancho.

With the blueberry muffins in their backpacks,
the three boys started for school.

On the way they met a football player from the

high school team.

"Do you guys
play ball?"
he asked.
They said they did.

"Okay, go deep!"

"Way to go, little man!" said the football player.

"You're pretty fast.
I have a sister
your age—she's
fast too."

Henry knew his sister.

He thought she was the loveliest girl in his class.

Her name was Chloe.

She sat in the back row.

"Are you looking at me?" Chloe asked.

For lunch Henry had
a peanut butter sandwich,
an apple, and a carton of
milk. He would save the
blueberry muffin for
afternoon snack.

At recess Henry decided to walk up to Chloe. "You're not going to talk to a *girl*, are you?" said Sancho.

Henry did his best forward roll.

"Show him what you can do, Chloe," said Abby.

Chloe turned a perfect cartwheel.

Henry was impressed.

"You're it!" A boy named Leonard tagged Henry.

The chase was on!

"You will *never* catch me!" said Chloe.

Back in class Mrs. Devine announced it was time to change

the seating arrangements. "Billy, you will sit here . . .

"And Chloe, please move your desk next to Henry's."

Now it was time for snack.

"What did you bring?" Chloe asked.

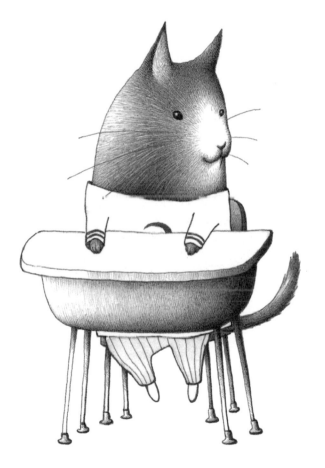

"Wow, thank you, Henry!"

Chloe ate the blueberry muffin.

Henry had a carrot.

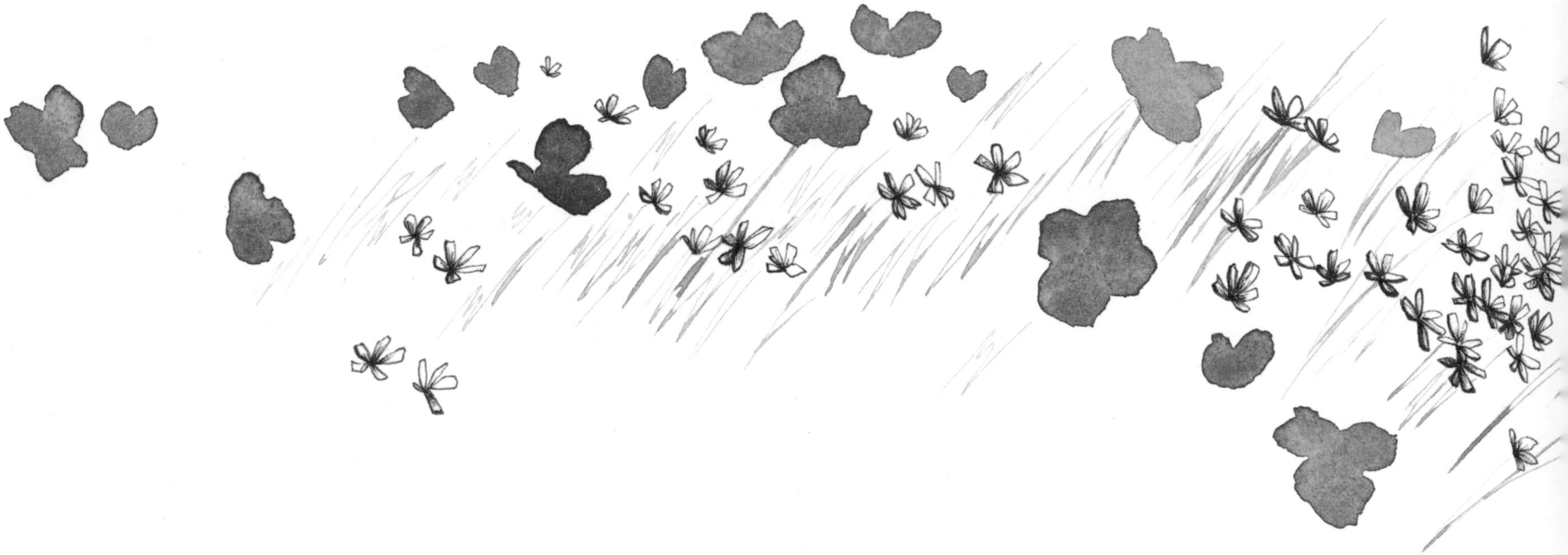